THE STORM WHALE in WINTER

With thanks
to Nia, Lara & Jane.

SIMON AND SCHUSTER
First published in Great Britain in 2016 by
Simon and Schuster UK Ltd, 1st Floor,
222 Gray's Inn Road, London WC1X 8HB
A CBS Company • Text and illustrations copyright
© 2016 Benji Davies • The right of Benji Davies to
be identified as the author and illustrator of this
work has been asserted by him in accordance
with the Copyright, Designs and Patents Act,
1988 • All rights reserved, including the right
of reproduction in whole or in part in any
form • A CIP catalogue record for this book is
available from the British Library upon request
Printed in Italy • ISBN: 978-1-4711-1997-2
(HB) • ISBN: 978-1-4711-1998-9 (PB) • ISBN:
978-1-4711-1999-6 (eBook) • 10 9 8 7 6 5 4 3 2

THE STORM WHALE
in WINTER

Benji Davies

SIMON AND SCHUSTER
London   New York   Sydney   Toronto   New Delhi

Noi lived with his dad and six cats by the sea.

Last summer, Noi rescued a little whale after a storm washed it ashore. He and his dad took it back to the sea, where it belonged.

But Noi could not forget his friend.

Now and then he thought he caught a glimpse
of the whale, its tail tipping the waves in the distance.

But it was always something else.

Winter was setting in, and all around the island the sea slowly filled with ice.

Noi's dad took one last trip in his fishing boat.

But when darkness fell that evening, his dad was still not home and Noi began to worry.

Noi watched and waited,
waited and watched.

Suddenly he saw something
out at sea.

It was his dad - it had to be!

He counted all six cats safe inside
and dashed down to the shore.

Noi dragged his boat to the water's
edge but the sea was frozen hard.

"I must be careful!" he thought,
stepping out on to the thick ice.

The further Noi went the harder
the snow fell, until everywhere
looked the same.

Noi was lost!

Then up ahead he saw
a grey shape flickering
in the lamplight.

It was his dad's boat stuck in the ice.
Noi quickly clambered aboard.

"Dad?" Noi called.

But his voice echoed – the boat was empty.

Noi didn't know what to do. As he curled up tight
he imagined the deep sea swirling beneath him
and he began to feel afraid.

Then through the darkness, the boat went BUMP!

It was the storm whale.

The whole family had come to help Noi.

The whales pushed their noses
into the cold night air.

They sang through puffs of steam and spray
as the ice cracked and crunched.
Somehow they knew where to go.

The little boat thumped hard against the rocks.
"Dad!" cried Noi.

"Noi! What are you doing here?" said his dad.
"I just had to find you!" said Noi.

As winter turned slowly to spring they often spoke of that cold, icy night.

The night the fishermen had rescued Dad,
and the storm whale had rescued Noi.

And Noi would smile . . .

. . . because it was the night
his friend came back.